RISING WALLS

CONNOR WHITELEY

No part of this book may be reproduced in any form or by any electronic or mechanical means. Including information storage, and retrieval systems, without written permission from the author except for the use of brief quotations in a book review.

This book is NOT legal, professional, medical, financial or any type of official advice.

Any questions about the book, rights licensing, or to contact the author, please email connorwhiteley@connorwhiteley.net

Copyright © 2024 CONNOR WHITELEY

All rights reserved.

DEDICATION

Thank you to all my readers without you I couldn't do what I love.

CHAPTER 1

Queen Augusta Windsoro stood on the wonderfully hard, perfectly smooth cobblestone pavement of her own breath-taking royal gardens as she waited for her latest royal appointment to arrive. Some ambassador from one of the two remaining human kingdoms. Augusta hardly cared which.

The sun was perfectly high in the crystal clear blue sky so it shone like a bright beacon of hope, happiness and good fortune over her kingdom of Octogi and Lordigo and she was so glad the weather was good.

The cobblestone pavement she was standing on was lined with large sensational bushes of fresh blue roses, and as much as Augusta loved her royal gardens it was the roses that really did it for her. On the bushes there were so many large roses that it was stunning to look at.

She really wished that she could spend all day and night in the gardens exploring the trees, plants and flowers that came from all four of the old human kingdoms. And ever since Augusta had claimed Lordigo through peaceful means, she had managed to add even more delightful plants to her ever-growing collection.

The air was always a dazzling combination of sweet fresh roses, sharp bitter apples that grew in an orchard just behind the rose trees and the sweet citrus bite of the blood oranges that always left the sensational taste of orange tarts form on her tongue.

Augusta really loved her gardens more than almost any other part of the kingdom, and it was on days like this that she seriously needed the gardens more than ever.

It had been two great years since she had killed old King Alfred of Lordigo and his sons had agreed to join forces with her so the kingdoms merged. And Augusta was really enjoying having sexy, hot and stunning Charleston around and it was great how close they had grown over the past two years.

The union had been great for both countries. Octogi finally got a working sanitation system, money and reinforcements to defend the country from the constant threat of ork invasions. Everything had been great.

But the most powerful of the human kingdoms was clearly scared of Augusta's ambition and of course, the Emperor of Jasper had every single right to be concerned. She wanted all the human kingdoms under one united banner considering how many dangers there were.

Augusta believed she had done a great job in the first year of convincing Jasper and the Longmano Crown Prince that she was no threat to them, yet, and Jasper had even withdrawn the millions of soldiers, steam-powered tanks and creatures from the border as a gesture of peace.

Augusta still couldn't believe she had been so stupid to believe him and fall into the Emperor's trap. He wasn't waging a military war against her (even though she would have been crushed in a month or two), he was waging a political war against her kingdoms.

Jasper had cut off all trade with them, leading Octogi to be starving, many of Lordigo's fishing and other main industries were crippled because Jasper was no longer trading with them and even the religious leaders of the kingdoms were aligning themselves with Jasper.

Augusta hated those pathetic leaders anyway.

And to make everything even worse, Augusta really hated how the orks had taken a chunk of territory out of her kingdom last month. They had attacked three days after Lordigo and her own kingdom had merged and ever since she had been able to defeat them until now.

Augusta knew the moment that news got out, her people would be frightened, fearful and they would want her out immediately.

She knew that her damn rule was hanging by a

single thread so she just really, really hoped that whatever ambassador was coming to see her would have good news to share.

"Your majesty. The Ambassador of Longmano is here," Augusta's best friend and Chief Witch Savannah said.

Augusta really wanted Savannah to stay so Augusta could hear her input but Savannah smiled and went away, so clearly she had scanned the ambassador's mind and they were a good person who didn't want to kill her.

That was always good to know.

A few moments later a very tall man wearing bright yellow robes walked up to Augusta and bowed. She had heard stories of Longmanoians before and this one seemed different.

All her spies had confirmed that the Longmanoians were strong, muscular people that were extremely well-fed so they had good food, they were always attractive and never showed a single sign of injury.

This one wasn't like that.

Augusta weakly smiled at the man's burnt face that twisted into a half-smile because the other half had melted closed, but the man's eyes were so gentle, calm and caring that Augusta knew that he wasn't a danger.

He was wearing the official robes of Longmanoian government and it seemed so strange that he didn't bring any guard, treasure or anything with him.

Then Augusta noticed his shoes that looked to be black, finely crafted and bound together with some sort of golden thread that was all twisted and cracked and burnt.

"Your highness I have an urgent matter to discuss with you because the fate of the entire human lands rest on us two,"

Augusta frowned because this man certainly knew how to make an entrance but she knew that he wasn't lying. Over the past two years of the other two kingdoms getting more and more powerful, she had had so many meetings with lying politicians and she was a master now.

This man wasn't lying.

And that actually excited her a lot more than she ever wanted to admit.

CHAPTER 2

Charleston Alfred absolutely had to admit that sexy Augusta always knew exactly how to make his day even more interesting. After two wonderful years of advising the Queen and his precious brother on how to run both kingdoms, he had finally set up a new role for himself as a sort of military leader but clearly the world had other ideas.

He sat on a very cold and nobbly wooden chair next to beautiful Augusta's, who was sitting on a smaller version of her golden throne, with other captains, diplomats and other important people surrounding the Longmano ambassador.

Charleston had to admit that like so much of Octogi since the two kingdoms merged, the chamber they were in was so much better. The walls weren't dirty, foul and covered in black dirt. The walls were now perfectly polished and clean and Charleston could now see the colour of the stone was dark grey.

It looked so wonderful.

And even the air of the country was great with hints of pine, roasted rosemary and juicy pork filling it from the local shops. It was amazing what a good sanitation system could do.

The sound of the other important people talking, muttering and making stupid guesses about what the ambassador could be about to say just made Charleston laugh. It was great to see everyone was excited again after all the chaos of recent weeks and the secret loss of land to the orks, but Charleston was hoping beyond hope that this was good news not bad.

But he knew that was just sheer fantasy.

This was going to be very, very bad news.

Charleston had to admit that Augusta did look sensational today with her long raven hair flowing over her strong shoulders, her fit sexy body was loosely covered by an angelic white dress because of the summer heat and her features were so sharp and dazzling.

He so badly wanted to kiss her but he couldn't do that yet, no matter how badly both of them wanted to do exactly that.

"Is everyone here?" Augusta asked.

Everyone nodded and then she gestured the ambassador to start talking, and Charleston was surprised that it took him another minute to actually get started.

"My name is ambassador Lordo. This isn't easy to explain but my kingdom is dying and your kingdom is next," he said.

Charleston nodded about the name. It wasn't a real or fake name per se, it was most of a title and everyone who became an ambassador for the kingdom of Longmano was given that name and their old identity was erased from history.

An idea that both fascinated and scared Charleston.

"My Kingdom as you know your highness is like yours in the sense that we protect the human lands from trolls, goblins and other foul creatures that threat us from the south,"

Charleston and Augusta both nodded. He had visited Longmano a few times with his father and he had visited the makeshift border and military base that they used to stop the creatures from coming across. It was a weak defence but it was a defence nonetheless.

And as much as Charleston hated to admit it, it was still probably a better defence than their one against the orks.

"But two months ago, we were attacked by a brand-new creature. It had the scales of a dragon, the body of a troll and the mind of a demon. It wasn't natural and our witches decided that it only could have been created by your kingdom or Jasper,"

Everyone gasped.

"Your excellence," Augusta said standing up. "I can assure you that is impossible. We did not create such a creature and I will admit I have no idea how it would even be done,"

The entire room looked at Savannah who was sitting the other side of Augusta and she weakly smiled.

"I have read about some things but I am, not exactly creative enough to do such a thing," she said.

Lordo smiled and Charleston was impressed he still managed to mock Savannah's admission of weakness but still have enough strength to stand.

Savannah hated to be mocked, and Charleston knew that from personal experience.

"To make matters worse, the new creature has two friends and it is the three of them that had invaded Longmano and attacked our capital. The King, Queen and Crown Princess are all dead and devoured,"

Everyone went silent.

"We sent word to Jasper hoping for aid. Three days later our emissaries were shipped to the palace in chunks with a piece of ribbon attached from Jasper,"

Charleston slammed his fist into the table and Augusta gave him a sideways glance.

"The Crown Prince lives," Lordo said before turning to Charleston, "but as your brother can attest. The Crown Prince cannot be king under the laws of the Gods,"

Charleston was pleasurably shocked when he felt Augusta place a loving hand on his leg as Charleston bit his own tongue so hard that it bleed ever so slightly.

He absolutely hated the deluded belief that just

because his brother was gay, he couldn't be king under any circumstances. It made Charleston just laugh as his brother Owen was ruling Lordigo in Augusta's name and it was quickly becoming one of the most powerful kingdoms in history.

Both Octogi and Lordigo were in a literal golden age because of the amazing work of his brother and Augusta.

"So I am here to request your support and… maybe you visiting the kingdom to see if you can help us pick a new ruler. And yes I am asking this despite your ultimate ambition,"

Charleston had to admit Lordo wasn't stupid. He knew that Augusta would use this opportunity to claim Longmano for herself and he really wanted to her to do it.

But if so much of the country was destroyed, devoured and ruled by the creatures of the south. Then Charleston really didn't know how useful they would be.

Especially as the bells of the ork's ultimate invasion got louder and louder as Charleston knew it was only a matter of time before the orks finally broke through.

And the orks would kill them all.

CHAPTER 3

Augusta seriously loved being queen of the second largest kingdom in all of the human lands because it meant she was powerful, kind and she did actually love helping innocent people. And as far as she was concerned the people of Longmano were very innocent.

Augusta pressed her back against the perfectly warm gold of the smaller version of her throne as she stared at Lordo. She still didn't like his yellow robes that made him look like a so-called sun and symbolise he was a force of good. That remained to be seen but she did want to listen to him.

The air smelt great with hints of refreshing pine, rosemary and freshly roasted pork from the lunchtime business of the amazing people of the capital city that left the delightful taste of succulent pulled pork sandwiches on her tongue.

Augusta looked at Lordo for a moment and she was ever so impressed with him. It was very ballsy of him coming to her in such a way knowing that she did want to conquer his kingdom.

Well, she knew that conquer was the wrong word because she only wanted him to join the kingdom of Octogi through peaceful and willing means, and he had just given her the perfect excuse and the perfect way for Longmano to join her kingdom in a fashion.

If wonderful Owen and the Crown Prince fell in love, got married then there was a political argument that meant Augusta would rule over the country. Of course the argument would be made unbreakable if her and Charleston were married.

But as much as she loved him because of his sensational body, intelligence and kindness she hadn't even made a move on him yet. But having him sitting next to her felt so right, perfect and natural.

"Where is the Crown Prince now?" Augusta asked.

Lordo shook his head. "Your highness, no disrespect but I do not *trust* anyone that is not Longmanoian. I will not reveal the location of someone so important,"

"How can he be so important if you admit you dislike him because of his choice of love?" Charleston asked a lot harsher than Augusta would have liked.

Lordo snarled at him. "I have no problems with gays Charleston of Lordigo. My own brother and sister were gay before the trolls killed them. I only wish that the Crown Prince wasn't so we could marshal some kind of response,"

"And there's the truth," Augusta said.

Everyone else in the room nodded slowly as they started to understand exactly why Lordo was here, why he was so scared and ultimately why he was injured.

"When did the riots start? Who is in control? What did Jasper spread?" Augusta asked so kindly that even she was impressed with herself.

Lordo snarled. "They invaded first of all. They assassinated the King's royal guards. It was nothing at first really, then these new creatures turned up and then they wiped out everyone in charge,"

Augusta weakly smiled at him gesturing that he had her full attention.

"I snatched the Crown Prince. He was so brave, he was fighting the trolls far better than his homophobic mother ever did but I snatched him and by the gods did I protect him,"

As Lordo gestured to his burnt features, Augusta nodded because she hated hearing this, but at least she knew just how dangerous Jasper was.

Augusta went out from around the wooden table and everyone gasped as she broke diplomatic protocol but she didn't care.

"This is no longer a fight for just Longmano. This is about the survival of our species and our way of life. Charleston can tell you then if your kingdom joins mine, then your culture, heritage and more will be protected I swear to you," Augusta said.

Lordo looked her dead in the eye but Augusta

didn't look away because she wasn't lying. She loved learning about other cultures, other heritages and exploring the history of Lordigo. It was such a rich kingdom and it was that culture that she wanted to protect for as long as she could.

Of course in the end, Lordigo culture would be combined with her own kingdom's and then Longmano's culture would combine and make it evolve even more. But that was a truly wonderful thing that Augusta was so damn excited about.

"Is she lying?" Lordo asked Charleston more of a challenge than a question without taking his eyes away from Augusta.

"No. She's actually preserved it far better than King Alfred ever did,"

Lordo nodded. "You are not wrong about our survival and Jasper will kill us all in the end so yes, when we return to Longmano I will talk to the Crown Prince about releasing his claim to the throne and requesting you take it,"

Augusta didn't like that idea at all because she had read a lot about Longmanoians in recent months and they were seriously obsessed with their monarchy. The common people didn't care about the Crown Prince being gay, that was only the religious leaders, so as long as the Crown Prince lived the people would always want him over her.

So the marriage idea was Augusta's only plan forward.

"Savannah," Augusta said, "please make

preparation for coming with us to Longmano and I'll send Cargo to tell Owen we're coming to collect him as well,"

Augusta was so excited about this trip, seeing her dragon Cargo since they had met for breakfast earlier and she was finally going to see precious Owen again.

Lordo smiled and then the entire room became a hive of activity as everyone prepared to march for Longmano.

But Augusta couldn't deny the twisting of her stomach as she wondered just how much the orks were preparing for their own attack.

Yet Longmano falling to Jasper, trolls and more horrors had to be the more immediate threat.

It just had to be.

CHAPTER 4

As Charleston, beautiful Augusta and Owen rode in the large golden carriage, Charleston really couldn't believe just how much tension there was. Well, it might have been tension per se but Owen purposefully had his head inside the latest book of a politics series he had been devouring for months, and Charleston really didn't want to speak until he had to.

The interior of the carriage was wonderful and it was amazing what happened when the engineering might of Octogi and the sheer beautiful textiles of Lordigo were combined.

This royal carriage was a lot less bumpy and stronger than anything he had ridden when his dick of a father was alive, but it was also more beautiful than Augusta's old one.

Charleston really loved the wonderfully soft velvety fabrics that covered the seats lovingly and they provided just enough comfort to make the trip a lot nicer without going overboard and making

Charleston feel like he was riding in some child-proof box.

Even the air smelt delightful with hints of roses, lilacs and lavender filling his senses and leaving the sweet taste of ham sandwiches form on his tongue from his childhood when his mother would sneak him and Owen off into the gardens for a picnic.

She always was a great mother, it was just a shame that his father killed her.

As the carriage went over a very large pothole, Charleston looked out the thin glass window and he was very impressed with the thick forests of Longmano. The trees were like immense soldiers towering over the land they protected.

Their branches had to be like massive swords ready to smite anyone who dared to invade their holy land, and it was just a shame that these mighty trees hadn't been able to defend most of the country.

Charleston and the others had flown here on the breath-taking back of Cargo, Augusta's beautiful dragon, but Augusta had ordered her best dragon friend to wait in case the Longmanoians hated dragons. She never ever wanted to put her friends in danger, human or otherwise.

"You're worried," Charleston said to beautiful Augusta at last and she didn't even look at him.

Instead she simply focused on the passing trees. "They say in a hundred or so years this will be something called a rainforest,"

Charleston nodded. He had read the same

reports and they sounded like beautiful things, apparently the elves had them as well.

"Jasper is what is concerning me. I know the Emperor is as ambitious as me when it comes to ruling but creating creatures to destroy Longmano. That is a new low even for him. We cannot fail,"

Charleston nodded. It was one of the reasons he loved her, she was always thinking about other people and what was best about her subjects. At end of the day he truly believed that she would sacrifice herself for her people.

Her life probably didn't matter that much to her in comparison to their lives. But to Charleston she was worth the world.

"I'm still not thrilled about a political marriage," Owen said.

And now Charleston knew what book he was reading. He couldn't exactly say he was thrilled either about the idea of marrying off his brother to a random crown Prince for the sake of power.

But it wasn't just about power. It was about making sure the kingdoms of Octogi, Lordigo and Longmano were strong enough to stand against Jasper. The kingdom that would conquer and kill them all in the end.

"You could be silly and believe Lordo's plan will work," Augusta said.

"You don't think the Crown Prince will give you the crown?" Charleston asked.

"Of course they won't," Owen said. "Those

people are far too dedicated to the Crown Prince for that. I understand it because, he is cute but Longmanoians have a zealous devotion to their monarchy,"

Charleston loved it how his brother was so clever and it was even better when Augusta looked at him for the first time in hours. She was so beautiful.

"Exactly. I've bought Savannah with us in case we can defeat these monsters and get an alliance that way,"

Charleston shook his head. "This sounds like a lot of guessing and hoping,"

Augusta laughed. "It's how being queen works most of the time. You keep stumbling along until you find two very intelligent people to help you,"

Charleston mockingly bowed and the three of them laughed.

"But I will be clear about one thing," Augusta said, "Longmano is a country in ruin. It is a corpse and the sharks are very much circling for the final kill and to ravage the body. I don't know if you're sharks or prey yet,"

Charleston simply nodded because he completely agreed. There was a lot more going on here than they could possibly understand for now.

New creatures weren't just created or born. If Jasper were the creators of such monsters then Charleston hated to imagine what they had install for Augusta.

Their real enemy.

CHAPTER 5

A few hours later, Augusta was really pleased to finally meet the amazing Crown Prince but she was a little more, shocked at the festival he had planned in her honour.

Augusta sat next to the Crown Prince and Charleston on the other side of her, on very cold and old and brittle stone chairs that were at least a thousand years old and that certainly showed in how a sharp piece of rock was stabbing her back.

The three seats were on top of a stone raised platform that had three awfully chipped steps down onto another raised stone platform that made sure that the people on it didn't have to touch the foul wet, damp rainforest ground.

Augusta really understood why they didn't want to touch it, she had already seen twenty different snakes with different venomous markings try to climb the platform more than once. Thankfully a kind of magical barrier stopped them but Augusta really wanted to go now.

Something bad was about to happen. She knew it.

There were three rows of wonderful stone tables on the platform below her, each one was covered in riches, food and amazing spices that made the air smell so richly of heaven and her mouth salivated at the sensational tastes forming on her tongue.

The sound of loud cheerful sound echoed around the rainforest as a small band of women sang, danced and clapped.

The atmosphere was so alive with joy, happiness and celebration that she was here and Augusta didn't know what at all to feel. She felt pleased that she was so well-liked but she still couldn't get over the feeling that something very, very bad was about to happen.

The Crown Prince seemed nice enough and Lordo had hugged him when they reunited, and the Prince was highly taken by Owen. The two of them had clicked instantly and spoken about every single little thing from politics to ruling kingdoms to being the sons of homophobic parents.

Apparently there was a hell of a lot to talk about in all forms.

And as much as Augusta had tried to talk to the Prince about business, he had really tried to have a normal conversation with her.

It wasn't until now that she understood why. Because the entire kingdom of Longmano hadn't had a reason to celebrate or be joyous for so long.

Everyone just wanted to enjoy these precious moments but the Crown Prince did promise an official meeting in a little while.

Augusta believed him.

Ya having fun there.

Augusta nodded as Cargo's words echoed in her mind and it was so good to feel his warm presence in her mind. They were connected and bonded in a way that Augusta was fairly sure she would never understand but she did love him like a best friend.

And I love you too as a friend only, of course girly.

Augusta laughed as she had forgotten that he could read her thoughts so easily and it was probably one of the reasons why she tried to think dirty about sexy Charleston.

"We need to have a party like this at home," Charleston said.

"Agreed but," Augusta said looking around to see if anything was strange, "do you feel like we're being watched?"

Charleston smiled and gestured to the partying people below them.

Augusta shook her head. "No. I mean-"

"Thank you everyone," the Crown Prince said in his stunning silver battle armour as he stood up and waved at the crowd. Everyone cheered at him and Augusta finally realised just how popular he was.

And it was also more than that.

Augusta understood and studied the faces of the people, they were happy because he was their leader, their constant and their connection to a past that they loved.

"This is a mighty moment for all of us," he said. "This is the moment when Longmano stands up to Jasper at last. My father would want me dead for saying this, but the future is not Jasper. The future is with Lordigo and Octogi,"

Everyone cheered in utter mania. Augusta felt her stomach twist into a painful knot. Something was very, very wrong.

"And it is tonight that I will finally announce and decree that Longmano is no more. Instead we are now the forever faithful subjects of Queen Augusta. She is fair, just and-"

"Traitor!" someone shouted.

Augusta had thought it was someone at the tables it wasn't. It was a pathetically short man in a long black cloak walking up the stone stairs from the rainforest floor and the snakes were following him. A black hood covered his face.

There was no more magical barrier.

"Emergency extraction requested," Augusta said in a whisper.

Confirmed.

"For too long have the monarchy dictated our actions and you have become blinded by your own weakness. Now I have come to save this country and take it for myself," the cloaked man said.

The Crown Prince pointed at him. "You, Lord Sacaden are the traitor. You have twisted, shattered and broken your oaths too many times for me to forgive you like my father did,"

The man took off his hood and Augusta screamed. The man's face was constantly moving, twisting and screaming with the ghosts of murdered victims.

"You know who I am then," Lord Sacaden said. "Then it will only make your death easier,"

Augusta and Charleston and Owen stood up as one single unit and whipped out their swords.

Sacaden laughed. "Die!"

The snakes shot forward.

CHAPTER 6

It was a bloodbath.

Charleston absolutely hated this foul Lord Sacaden as the massive snakes shot forward and seemed to grow three times larger. Charleston knew Augusta was clever enough to order Cargo to collect them.

But until then they were alone. The royal guards weren't here. Augusta's forces were all far south looking at the troll invasion and Savannah was unknown.

He so badly wanted her to be okay.

The snakes roared as they zoomed towards their prey. They sunk their fangs into the necks of innocent people.

People screamed.

Charleston wiped out his sword. Charging forward.

Snakes hissed at him.

Charleston charged forwards.

He swung at the enemy.

His sword slicing their flesh.

The snakes grew bigger.

Charleston slashed at them. Lash at their throats.

The snakes grew bigger. And bigger.

Charleston shot back towards Augusta.

Lord Sacaden launched fireballs at them.

A snake attacked Charleston.

Launching itself at him.

Charleston tried to kill it.

The snake slammed him against the stone chairs.

The chairs shattered.

Deadly stone shards sliced through the air.

A magical shield formed around Augusta.

Charleston leapt up.

Savannah appeared on the edge of the platform. Her golden staff crackled.

Sacaden laughed at her.

He charged at her.

Charleston flew at the traitor Lord.

A snake tripped him.

Charleston rolled over.

The snake about to strike. Owen jumped in front.

Slicing the snake.

It only grew bigger.

Charleston leapt up.

Rushing over to Augusta. He had to protect her.

Savannah screamed.

Magical firestorms exploded.

The two magic users slaughtered each other.

Their magic matched. No one managed to beat each other.

Charleston stared in terror.

All the snakes wrapped around each other.

Becoming a single immense snake.

The snake dived at them.

Charleston grabbed his friends. He threw them onto the rainforest floor.

Owen leapt up first. Charleston grabbed Augusta.

Charleston couldn't see the Prince.

A deafening screamed ripped through the rainforest.

The snake melted away.

Charleston dashed up the platform.

Owen rushed past him.

He cradled the Prince in his arms. A massive bite to the neck made deep red blood gush out of the wound.

The Prince screamed in pain.

Charleston went to the Prince and Augusta knelt down next to him.

"Go to the Prison rock," the Prince said gripping Augusta's hand. "I name you Queen damn you,"

Charleston was shocked that the Prince wasn't mad or angry about at Augusta or anything. He was angry at the world, himself and most importantly Sacaden.

The howling of tens of humans echoed all around them as the Prince died and Charleston,

Owen and Augusta stood up to see tens of chieftains of tribes and clans step onto the platform and breathe in the air.

Like this was holy fresh air that they had never ever been allowed to breathe before.

Charleston recognised tons of the tribal markings, it should have been impossible for these tribes to be working together.

But it was happening. Somehow this Lord Sacaden had united all the tribes that the royal family of Longmano had outcasted and now they were a single fighting force ready to take Longmano for themselves.

And Charleston realised something he should have realised ages ago.

Jasper hadn't created any of these conditions or creatures. It was the tribes that somehow became so powerful that they could create brand-new deadly creatures.

All the chieftains whipped out their knives as Savannah screamed and Sacaden placed her into a headlock.

Augusta went forward but Charleston gripped her elbow. This wasn't the time for friendships.

This was only the time for survival.

"I'll come back for you," Augusta said and Savannah nodded.

The Chieftains charged.

Rising their swords.

Cargo roared in utter fury.

Torrents of fire rained down upon the enemy.

People screamed.

Cargo whacked Sacaden with his tail and landed.

Charleston, Augusta and Owen didn't even hesitate. They all rushed aboard and Cargo flew away.

As Charleston watched Savannah nod at him, he knew that tonight had gone horrifically wrong.

And they had just stumbled into a much greater threat than he ever thought possible for such an annihilated kingdom.

CHAPTER 7

As Cargo landed, Augusta, Charleston and Owen climbed down and landed on the awfully hard rocky ground of a very tall hill that was like a spire rising out of the rainforest like a watchtower over the territory. It didn't exactly look like it was easy to climb up so Augusta just hoped that would be enough to protect them for now.

She had never seen such a massacre before and she had utterly hated it. So many innocent people slaughtered, the Crown Prince assassinated and now her best friend in the entire world was captured.

She absolutely hated to imagine what poor Savannah was going through, Augusta only wanted her to be okay.

Cargo rose up and reared his head higher than she had ever seen him before, at least he was studying the rainforest and probably using his dragon senses to protect them. Augusta was more than glad about that.

Augusta went over to Charleston and Owen who

were sitting down on the cold dark damp rock of the hill, and she joined them. She knew that she was extremely lucky to have such wonderful people in her life but their faces said it all.

They didn't have a clue what to do, but Augusta always prided herself on being a loving, caring and generous queen so right now Owen was her top priority.

"Are you okay?" Augusta asked placing a loving hand on Owen's cold armour.

He shook his head. "I had only known him for a few hours but he was a good man, a good leader and he, he was going to help his people live better lives,"

"Did you love him?" Charleston asked carefully.

Owen shrugged. "It was a few hours but maybe one day. That is why we need a plan. We cannot return to our kingdoms like nothing has happened,"

Augusta couldn't deny that, because she had seen the rage, hunger and murderous intent of those monstrous chieftains. They wanted blood and corpses to pile up so she had no doubt that in the end the chieftains and whoever Sacaden was, they would come for her kingdoms.

Something she absolutely couldn't allow.

"He mentioned something about Prison Rock. What is it?" Augusta asked.

The men shrugged and she supposed that was to be expected. None of them were from Longmano so a top-secret rock could be anything. It could be an actual rock, a bar or a hotel for all she knew.

"It has to be something very important," Owen said. "I don't think he was the sort of man to say random stuff on his death bed,"

A loud hiss echoed through the rainforest. Trees moved in the distance.

Augusta looked at Cargo and her beautiful dragon shook his head so at least they had a little time before the immense snake caught up with them.

"What about our people at the palace?" Charleston asked.

That was a great question and Augusta loved how the beautiful man was thinking so clearly about what was going on despite her own chaotic brain.

"Captured," Cargo said like it was nothing but Augusta knew he was focusing on the rainforest more than them.

"We're alone," Owen said. "We need to travel south into the troll-controlled lands, the Prince mentioned of a wizard in the caves that was some somewhat loyal to him from time to time,"

"Somewhat?" Augusta asked, grinning.

Another loud hiss ripped through the rainforest. Time was running out.

"The wizard and the Prince had a secret love affair for a few months. Then the King found out and cut off the wizard's arms,"

Augusta nodded. That would certainly make a person's loyalties touch and go for the rest of their life.

"My Lady," Cargo said before roaring into the air

and the loud hissing of thousands of snakes hissing got deafening.

Everyone got up and they all climbed up Cargo. The enemy had found them as Cargo raced off towards the troll-controlled areas Augusta just knew that things were going to get a lot worse before they got better.

Augusta just had to protect her people, the man she loved and his precious brother. No matter the cost.

And there was always a cost in the end.

CHAPTER 8

A few hours later when Cargo landed in a very small valley with immense steep sloping sides made of glowing pink rock with the mountain range in front of them, Charleston absolutely hated the coughing air. It felt so thick, toxic and corrupt that even his lungs seemed to protest to him breathing but he forced himself to breathe.

He couldn't protect the woman he loved and his wonderful brother if he didn't breathe.

Charleston looked up at the immense mountain that Cargo had dropped them off in front of and it was rather imposing. He had climbed mountains and hiked through vast trails as a teenager on the snowy mountains of Lordigo but the sharp dagger-like rocks of this mountain were something else.

The mountain stood at twice the height of any mountain he had climbed as a teenager and even then the Lordigo mountains had been like giants. Thick blankets of snow cloaked the tops so the mountain could have been even taller.

The pink glowing rock the valley was made from disappeared as soon as it touched the mountain to be replaced with black shiny rock that felt awful and looked to be flaking at an alarming rate.

Charleston wouldn't have been surprised if it was impossible to climb but they needed to.

They all took out their swords in case they were attacked because they had already drawn the attention of troll and goblin and shadowy demon patrols. Whoever was in charge of these forces clearly knew how to run a military, and no troll could do that.

Augusta stood on the mountain and Charleston joined her then Owen. The black rock of the mountain cracked slightly under all of their weight and the cracks spread up the mountain.

He really doubted this mountain was climbable but this was the only "safe" route up. Cargo had flown around the mountain five times and all the other routes were covered by trolls, demons or the rocks were simply too dangerous to climb up.

"We're friends of the Crown Prince!" Owen shouted.

Charleston grabbed him but Augusta waved him away and as much as Charleston didn't want to release his brother for doing something so stupid in enemy territory he complied with her command.

"Please don't do that again," she said. "But it's a clever idea. Let's hope the wizard heard it,"

"And doesn't want to kill us," Charleston said.

Owen raised his sword. Charleston spun around.

Tens of white-skinned goblins with little pop-bellies, pusy eyes and bend little metal swords descended on the valley.

"Well, well, well. Look what the trash bought in," the larger and fattest of the goblins said.

Charleston and Augusta raised their swords but he hated how Augusta was in danger. She wasn't a fighter and he had been teaching her for two years but she was still a rubbish fighter.

She was intelligent not a fighter.

"Let's gut up the humans!" the leader shouted.

The goblins charged.

The three of them formed a defensive line.

Cargo roared.

Unleashing a torrent of black fire.

Goblins screamed.

They cooked.

They died.

More goblins descended into the valley.

Cargo hissed.

The goblins were coming down the mountains.

Charleston flew at the goblins.

He swung his swords.

Chopping off heads.

Freeing Cargo.

Cargo swung his tail.

Charleston swung his sword.

Again and again.

Blood splashed up his armour.

Goblins were slaughtered.
A goblin leapt on his back.
Lashing at his neck.
Charleston hissed in pain.
He couldn't kill the goblin.
Cargo shot a fireball at him.
The goblin died.
More goblins jumped on Charleston.
There were too many.
They pulled him to the ground.
They slashed at his armour.
The goblins cackled at him.
They punched him.
Slashing his cheek.
More goblins pinned him to the ground.
Cargo screamed.
The goblins pinned down a dragon.
There were thousands of goblins now.

As Charleston heard the hissing of Owen and Augusta echo around the valley he just knew that they were done for and they were now prisoners of the goblin kingdom.

The largest and fattest of the goblins who had to be their leader jumped on Charleston's chest and Charleston coughed in pain. The goblin was a hell of a lump.

"Well well well. Pathetic little humans," the leader said slamming a small wooden club in his hands. "Night night little man,"

The goblin leader smashed the club into

Charleston's head.
    His world went black.

CHAPTER 9

When Augusta awoke, she seriously couldn't believe the foul aroma of poo, death and rotting flesh that slammed into her senses. She hated the smell with all her life and passion and when she stood up and her vision cleared, it hardly got any better.

She was standing on a cold wooden platform that seemed to be bound together with human hair, skin and teeth used as nails. The wooden platform was in the centre of a massive black rocky cavern in the heart of the mountain range.

There were other fouler wooden platforms hanging dangerously off the walls with thousands of goblins watching her, cheering and arguing amongst themselves in a language she didn't understand but it was probably about how she was going to die.

Augusta knew a lot about the goblins, she had taken a module on them at university but now she was facing them. She was utterly terrified and she really wished Savannah was here with her.

Augusta went to the edge of the wooden platform and she saw at the platform was suspended in the middle of the cavern with a very, very long drop to dagger-like rocks below her.

If the platform fell then she would die. There was no arguing with that simple truth.

"Ya know little human," a voice said echoing off the walls of the cavern and the goblins fell silent, some even shivered in fear. "That I have always wanted to kill a Queen,"

"You already killed a Crown Prince. I am no different," Augusta said.

She really wanted to know exactly where Charleston and Owen were but she didn't dare show she cared about them to the enemy.

"Correct, but we are not associated with Lord Sacaden. He is our enemy just as much as you are," the voice said.

Augusta realised the voice wasn't goblin at all. The voice was very, very human and she had absolutely no idea at all how the hell a human could control goblins.

Only an extremely dangerous person could.

"We are working to similar ends then," Augusta said looking around wanting to see the human.

The goblins laughed at her.

"I agree with the goblins," the voice said. "That is a silly thing to say. We want to rule the kingdom in the name of the goblin king and you wish to rule it for yourself. You do not wish the same as us,"

Augusta nodded. A lot of things were starting to make sense now and there were thankfully a hell of a lot more divisions than she realised earlier.

And divisions bought opportunity.

"She knows who the King is," a booming voice said.

The Goblins screamed, shouted and ran away, some falling off their platforms and getting killed on the rocky spikes below.

A shadowy black figure appeared and Augusta gripped a sword that wasn't there as Lord Sacaden appeared on the platform wearing his black cloak.

Augusta was just glad he had his hood up.

"Where's Savannah?" Augusta asked.

Someone smashed Augusta over the head.

She fell forward.

Falling over the edge of the platform.

Augusta barely managed to grip the edge of the platform so she didn't fall to her death.

Augusta bit her lip as she saw Savannah grinning at her like a madwoman.

Then Savannah and Lord Sacaden kissed like they were lovers.

"You are very stupid your highness. You are a fool. You never checked to see where I was born, were my love was and where my alliances laid,"

Augusta shook her head. This couldn't be true. Savannah was no traitor. She just couldn't be.

"Remember your highness how I left you with the ambassador. I did so because I had personally ordered Lordo not to hurt you. By the Gods did he want to but I stopped him,"

Augusta couldn't believe this. It just couldn't be true.

"Do you remember your highness how Lordo mocked my weak magic and I didn't kill him for mocking me? And yet I punish everyone else who mocks me,"

Augusta gasped. This could actually be true.

"Your highness," Savannah said kneeling down next to her. "Do you think it was weird how excited I was to travel to Longmano after how much I had come to hate travelling to other kingdoms?"

Augusta shook her head.

"Well I do. I hate this world. I hate you. And I will rule it all for myself,"

Lord Sacaden coughed and Savannah nodded.

"Of course I meant for me and Sacaden,"

Augusta smiled because that was another point of attack for her. They might have been lovers but they weren't in love unlike her and Charleston. There was a weakness in their relationship and Sacaden certainly didn't trust her.

Augusta had to use that to her advantage but she closed her eyes and focused on Cargo.

Her dagger mark on her hand glowed slightly and she knew that Cargo was alive. The goblins were guarding him outside and keeping him pinned.

But Cargo was simply buying time for when Augusta needed him most.

"Soon my dear," Augusta whispered and she felt Cargo send warming loving thoughts into her mind.

He would be ready and as a magical force gripped and pulled her back up onto the platform. She couldn't believe that Savannah placed her in handcuffs.

So many decades of friendship gone in a moment.

"And now we will kill the goblin king," Savanna said.

Augusta's stomach twisted into an agonising knot as she realised whoever killed the Goblin King not only ruled over the goblins but also ruled over the demons and every other evil magical creature except the trolls.

Lord Sacaden was about to get extremely powerful.

Augusta had to stop them. She just had no idea how to do it.

Not a clue at all.

CHAPTER 10

The foul aromas of charred flesh, smouldering corpses and death clung to the air like its life depended on it and Charleston hated it as it assaulted his senses. He was surprised that he wasn't chained up or anything.

He was simply laying on the damp wooden floor looking at rope made from human hair, teeth used as nails and skin used as reinforcing for the rope. It was a foul sight and Charleston really wanted to escape.

He forced himself to stand up and he was in a very small cavern made from black rock, there weren't any goblins about to his utter relieve but there was a phoenix popping about on human, ork and other skulls belonging to animals that Charleston really didn't know about.

He was even more surprised the phoenix seemed to be talking to Owen just fine and they looked to be having a great and rather light-hearted conversation despite being in handcuffs made from hair.

Charleston brushed his hands through his own hair and thankfully it was all still attached and so was Owen's.

A shot of pain rushed past him as Charleston realised he didn't know where Augusta was, he so badly wanted her to be okay but he had to focus for now. He had to make sure that him and Owen survived.

Owen gestured towards him. "And your majesty, this is my brother Duke Charleston,"

Charleston bowed only because he really hoped his brother was working on a play here.

The Phoenix constantly flicked its rather wonderful eyes between him and his brother then it made a sort of woodpecker sound.

"Of course I'm the more handsome one," Owen said. "But this is my brother and we can help you if you want,"

Charleston reached for his sword but the Phoenix laughed at him and flew over to another wall where their swords hang perfectly intact. That wasn't like the goblins at all.

"This is the Goblin King," Owen said.

Charleston just smiled. That couldn't be right. This creature wasn't even a Goblin.

"It turns out he killed the old king two hundred years ago and has been ruling the so-called Lesser Magical Creatures for hundreds,"

The Phoenix started making sounds again.

"I know. Sorry. Sorry. But I need to explain

things to my brother,"

"How can you talk to him?" Charleston asked.

Owen shrugged. "I have no idea. It's magic or some sort but the Phoenix seems interested in talking to me and me alone,"

"What's the problem and where's Augusta?"

The Phoenix laughed hard and Charleston felt the room go icy cold.

"The problem is that the King has foreseen his own death in a few moments. Augusta has already been captured by Savannah and Sacaden,"

Charleston stomped his foot. He went over to his swords and grabbed them.

The Phoenix made a bunch of sounds and even Owen seemed scared.

"He says that we need to go to Prison Rock. That is where the loyal Chieftains of the tribes, the village Eldermans and Ladies of Ancients are waiting to create a response,"

Charleston threw his arms up in the arm. "Where is the rock?"

He couldn't understand why Owen was closing his eyes and the Phoenix was leaning closer and as much as he wanted to kill the Phoenix in case he was harming his brother, he sort of just knew that if the Phoenix wanted them dead.

They would be already.

Owen opened his eyes and nodded. "I have the location but I cannot explain it. It's not a place per se, it's-"

The Phoenix screamed in utter agony as a fireball slammed into it and it was vapourised instead of turning to ashes so it could never be reborn and rise once more.

Charleston grabbed Owen and gave his brother a sword when Lord Sacaden walked in wearing his black cloak and hood and Savannah was holding Augusta in a very tight headlock.

"I do all of this because I want this kingdom to know true power.," Sacaden said. "When a person reaches 18 years old, I will test and if they have magic I will make them Lords and Ladies and give them the power they deserve. If not, I will enslave them like this kingdom enslaved me once,"

Charleston looked around for a means of escape but there wasn't one.

"This kingdom has been dying for so long that it was wonderful when I created new monsters to claim it for myself. So many people died, so many wizards and witches were freed and now the world will be mine,"

"You are deluded," Augusta said.

"Revenge is a powerful emotion my dear," Sacaden said. "This kingdom enslaved magic users. Our kingdoms do the same. Then I will go after the elves and dwarves, the only stupid creatures that could stop me and then I will be a God once more,"

Charleston shook his head. I could easily understand why Sacaden had wanted to free his people in Longmano but the kingdoms of Lordigo and Octogi now openly allowed witches and wizards to use their magic freely as long as it was used as a force for good.

A magical force gripped Charleston by the throat.

"And now you die," Sacaden said.

Charleston gasped for air. He couldn't breathe. He was choking.

His vision blurred.

His face went blue.

Something slammed into the mountains.

A dragon roared.

The temperature rose dramatically.

And Charleston realised they had a very fucked-off dragon on their hands.

CHAPTER 11

Augusta absolutely loved her amazing dragon best friend as the dagger burnt mark on her hand glowed golden and she felt Cargo's love, affection and raw power stream into her veins. He had to be leaning her some of his strength and magic and sheer force of rage as she felt the urge to kill Savannah or at least burn her arm around Augusta's throat.

She looked at Charleston. He nodded. He was ready so Owen was ready moments before.

Augusta imagined wings shooting off her back for a moment.

Savannah was thrown across the room. The wings disappeared.

Augusta charged forward.

Augusta's hands became claws.

She shot out fire.

Sacaden panicked.

He hissed in pain.

Fireballs slammed into him.

Owen slashed Sacaden's back.

He screamed.

Savannah slammed her golden staff on the ground.

Throwing Augusta against a wall.

The rock grew around her.

Augusta breathed out fire.

Melting the rock.

Savannah launched torrents of ice at Augusta.

Forcing her back.

Augusta smashed the ice away.

She was feeling weaker.

This fight had to end now.

Sacaden punched Charleston.

Shattering his nose.

Augusta flew forward.

Savannah grabbed her.

Whacking Augusta round the face with her staff.

Knocking out teeth.

Savannah slammed her staff into Augusta's legs.

She fell to the ground.

Savannah placed her staff over Augusta's throat.

She couldn't move.

Sacaden punched Owen and Charleston in the head and they collapsed to the ground. Augusta hated to imagine how messed up their vision was but they were defeated.

It was only because of Cargo's strength she had been able to fight. She wasn't much of a fighter but she was a skilled talker.

And talking bought time for help to arrive or for Charleston and Owen to come up with a new plan.

Augusta went to speak but no sound came out and Savannah laughed at her.

This had to be some kind of damn magic, and Augusta was so looking forward to killing Savannah.

"Where is Prison Rock?" Sacaden asked Owen. "I know it isn't a physical place. It is a psychic location,"

Augusta was surprised. That was extremely clever of the Longmanoians, it was completely brilliant to hide their last stronghold or whatever the rock actually was in its own pocket dimension or something.

"I do not know," Owen said.

Sacaden punched him.

Augusta tried to speak more and more and it looked like it was paining Savannah so Augusta realised that at least she could still hear what she was saying. That had to be enough for now.

"Do you really think he loves you? You are a nobody, a weak little girl that my father picked up off the streets out of pity. Do you think you were ever liked? Do you think Sacaden loves you?

Savannah bit her lower lip.

"You are nothing to anyone," Augusta said with any sound coming out. "Sacaden will kill you the first moment he gets because you are a pathetic little woman just wanting to play god for a little longer,"

Savannah grinned at her and her lips thinned.

"Do you think I didn't plan for that already? It is me that will kill him in a few moments because I am not silly and I am the real master around here. I created the creatures through Sacaden,"

Augusta didn't understand how that was possible at all.

"His mind was so rageful, weak and too easy to manipulate. Everything he thinks he has done and accomplished is actually my will made real,"

Augusta seriously couldn't understand how she had gotten her childhood best friend so very wrong.

"I'll prove it to you. I'll make him cut off his own left leg," Savannah said.

She clicked her fingers and nothing happened.

Sacaden started laughing and he punched Owen before turning on Savannah.

Augusta felt the magical sound-proof barrier around her disappear and Savannah gasped as if she was choking.

"Stupid woman," Sacaden said. "I was waiting for you to turn on me and now I tell you your reward for finally revealing yourself. Your childhood hometown of Lengtho is being raided as we speak,"

Savannah's lips thinned as this actually bothered her.

"All your magical mentors, teachers and everyone who ever bothered to care and love you will be slaughtered,"

"No!" Savannah shouted.

Magic energy shook the rocks and Augusta saw

her chance.

She leapt forward.

Tackling Savannah to the ground.

Charleston and Owen charged forward.

Smashing Sacaden over the head.

They all charged out the cavern.

Running down a narrow black rock corridor.

They didn't know where they were going.

Augusta ran into a large rocky cavern with thousands of goblins staring at her with their little swords raised.

This plan had also failed.

Augusta was tempted to shout for help or something but she was more concerned about why she hadn't heard or felt Cargo for ages.

The Goblins charged.

Augusta whipped out her sword.

Blinding golden light filled the cavern.

The goblins screamed.

A man in white robes gripped Augusta's wrist but she didn't struggle.

The man did the same to Charleston and Owen wrapped his arms around him.

Then the man teleported them away.

Augusta didn't know where to but she was done with damn goblins. She just hoped she hadn't replaced one monster for another.

RISING WALLS

CHAPTER 12

When the blinding golden light disappeared, Charleston was slightly more than shocked that him, beautiful Augusta and precious Owen were standing in the middle of a stone circle. It was beyond weird as there were stone seats with men and women sitting in sterile white robes just frowning at them.

There was a single spare stone seat and the sky was bright white and now Charleston realised that this was Prison Rock because the sky had to be magical in nature and even the air smelt too good to be true with hints of minty, vanilla ice cream and Augusta's perfume in the air.

If her sensational perfume wasn't so strongly in the air then Charleston might have believed this place wasn't living magic but he loved the smell too much for that to be a possibility.

The man in white robes smiled at each of them and Charleston could have sworn that he was looking at the ghost or something of the Crown Prince but the face changed to someone who had clearly lived a rough life.

The man's face was well-worn but kindly, friendly and he clearly wanted to help them. The man winked at Owen and Charleston realised this was the wizard friend of the Prince.

"Welcome to Prison Rock," the man said, "and Queen Augusta, a woman like us in more ways than one, I know that the Crown Prince named you queen but he is dead and we now rule,"

Charleston watched as Augusta laughed and studied each and every one of the people sitting on the chairs. He had no idea what she saw when she looked at them but to him, they all just looked like idiots focusing on a war of words when Sacaden was already wanting to come here and kill them all.

"What is this place really?" Augusta asked. "I have read books on magical architecture and forming pocket dimensions but this is remarkable. I guess there is a magical library, artefacts and more in this place,"

Everyone just frowned and some even spat at Augusta.

"I take that as a yes. It makes sense why this is such a threat to Sacaden. This place holds the knowledge, power and people that can stop him from taking Longmano,"

"And we will not allow you to do either!" a woman shouted.

Charleston looked at her. She was a very young

and beautiful woman with long blond hair and a black pin of some military rank on her robe.

"Calm down Jacinda," the wizard friend said.

"I will not," Jacinda said. "These people are just like Sacaden,"

Charleston laughed. "We are the only hope you have of defeating Sacaden. If you want to die then that's okay by me, just don't let your people die as the trolls and more invade your villages,"

Charleston loved it how Augusta gave him a slideway glance.

"These people must be killed immediately," Jacinda said. "These people are threats to Longmano,"

"Impossible," another person said.

"Hail Jacinda," another woman said.

Owen clapped his hands and everyone focused on him. Charleston really hoped Owen knew what he was doing.

The wizard friend of the Prince leant forward.

"This is a situation that is scary," Owen said. "I am scared, you are scared, your people are scared. This is a fight for all magical creatures so please listen to Queen Augusta and if you still don't like her then you can kill her,"

"Thanks Owen," Augusta said sarcastically.

Everyone on the stone seats nodded. Charleston really did love his brother and Augusta was so beautiful, but something about Jacinda just felt off.

"As my little gay friend said before he offered to

kill me, you are all the lords, ladies and wizards and witches of Longmano. Sacaden seeks to kill you all and he is coming here. We have to use that to our advantage,"

Jacinda stood up. "We can lure him here, access the knowledge and power of this place and then we can kill him once and for all,"

Charleston couldn't understand why Jacinda was being so active in this conversation and he could have sworn that the knowledge contained here was forbidden or something.

Then it clicked. Charleston whipped out his sword.

"Jacinda's working for Sacaden. She wants the knowledge opened so she can give it to him," Charleston said.

Everyone else denied it and called for Charleston to die but Jacinda just grinned.

"Of course I want to and now my plan can activate," she said.

The entire ground shook violently as it felt like the stone circle they were standing in had smashed into something.

The white magical sky disappeared and was replaced with their own sky. They were somewhere in Longmano.

Charleston looked at Jacinda's smouldering corpse, the sheer power to anchor the Prison Rock in reality must have killed her.

But as all the people in white robes stood up and

bowed to Augusta, he knew they finally had their support and now they had a lot of work to do.

Sacaden was coming and he wouldn't rest until he had the knowledge stored here and then he would kill them all and conquer the world.

CHAPTER 13

The icy cold breeze of the dying kingdom of Longmano lightly brushed Augusta's cheeks and she just smiled at the reminder that if she failed here then she was dead. As dead as a doornail.

Augusta stood just outside Prison Rock and even though its magic was all gone now because of the foul trickery that Jacinda had used, it was still an immense stalwart mountain of a rock that she was seriously hoping she could use to her advantage.

She was hardly sure about that. The mountain had screamed, moaned and groaned at being ripped into reality, and even the wizard friend of the Prince, who she now knew was called Jerry and he was also the leader of the people on the stone seats, had been concerned.

Jerry had mentioned repeatedly that the mountain's secrets normally opened themselves to him alone but the mountain was saying all sorts of things to him about how it was locking down.

Augusta hated that as she stared out onto the icy cold brown plane she found herself on. There was no cover, no help and no settlements around for hundreds of miles.

There would be no reinforcements here.

She could already see the shadowy outlines of demons running towards her out of the corners of her eyes. The enemy would be here far too soon for her liking and it really didn't help that the sun was setting.

Just like an immense fiery ball, the sun was disappearing in the east and she sadly knew this would be the final sunset for a lot of people on Prison Rock.

She wasn't blind to that fact but she had to protect as many of them as possible and she simply had to protect beautiful Charleston and precious Owen at all costs.

A lump formed in her throat as she realised that she had never kissed, hugged or even gestured to Charleston that she loved him. She really did. Augusta loved his kindness, his fighting style and just him. She had no idea what it was about his personality, his smile or his body that she loved so much.

But she loved him all the same.

Maybe before the end she would find a moment to tell him that but she didn't want him detracted during the fight. That would only make his, death a certainty.

Cargo's wings flapped as he landed and Augusta

laughed as her wonderful dragon snuggled his snout into her arms. Augusta kissed him lightly on the head.

"If anything happens," Augusta said, "you must live and take Charleston and Owen with you. I don't care if you have to snatch them. Just take them. Please,"

Cargo kissed her back as gently as a dragon could which wasn't very gentle.

"You don't know how being a Dragon Rider works, do you?"

Augusta shrugged. She was the first of such beings apparently, of course she had no idea how the hell they worked.

"If you die in battle then I die and you get my life force. You get to live a second life at my cost. I don't actually care. I would have that then lose you and I am the one that choose to bond with you after all,"

Augusta didn't dare speak. She didn't know what emotion could come out but things only seemed to be getting worse and worse and it was starting to kill her inside.

The entire world rested on her and she couldn't even save her friends and the man she loved.

"Charleston has finished establishing a perimeter," Cargo said sniffing the air like the scent of a deadly predator caught his nose.

"What's coming?"

Cargo laughed. "Everything is coming for us. And we need to get back inside,"

"What we need is that forbidden knowledge and

power and artifacts in the rock," Augusta said.

A deafening cheerful roar echoed around the rock and Augusta instantly recognised it as a demon's roar using a troll's voice box.

Those new creatures were here and they were coming to kill them.

Time had run out.

CHAPTER 14

Three lines of defence.

Charleston had absolutely no idea if it would be enough as he stood at the very end of a main black stone valley with steep slopes and dagger-like shards of rocks shooting out from the sides.

He really wanted this defensive position to hold and thankfully the witches and wizards of Prison Rock had managed to create large walls made of pure white magic crystal.

But as he felt Augusta who still looked stunning even now standing behind him, he really didn't want her here. She was a leader, not a fighter.

The sound of roaring, snarling and shouting echoed up the valley as the trolls, demons and other foul abominations got even closer and Charleston instantly knew they were heavily outnumbered.

He turned to Augusta. "You have to go to Stone Circle. Convince the mountain to share its secrets,"

Augusta looked like she wanted to fight or at

least say something.

Charleston grabbed her hands a lot harder than he ever meant to. He didn't let go.

"I love you but this isn't your place. You aren't a fighter. You're an amazing leader and your mind is what we need,"

Augusta slowly nodded and hugged him.

She was about to run up the valley when a loud cackling echoed up and down the valley as one.

Owen rushed over to Charleston and leapt over a crystal wall.

Both brothers whipped out their swords.

Charleston saw something dance in the darkness. It was like something was cloaked.

A troll appeared in front of Charleston.

Its skin turned into blood red dragon scales. Its club the size of most hills.

The troll swung it.

Charleston leapt to one side.

The club shattered the defences.

Demons laughed. Normal trolls stormed in.

Charleston swung at anything that moved.

Demons slashed at him.

Trolls kicked him.

Charleston fell back.

Slamming into rock.

Air rushed out his lungs.

He gasped for air.

A tall tree-like demon charged at him.

Owen came from nowhere.

Ramming his sword through the demon.

Air rushed back into Charleston's lungs.

He looked around. People were getting slaughtered.

White robes turned red. The headed became the headless.

Witches and wizards were being devoured by the new demon trolls.

Charleston shook his head. He hadn't seen the other two turn up.

He could hear them though.

All three trolls created by Sacaden were here so Sacaden wasn't far behind.

Charleston looked around.

Augusta slammed her sword into the head of a troll.

The troll swung at her.

Augusta leapt out the way.

The troll fell forwards.

Augusta jumped into the air.

Ramming her sword into the troll's head.

A demon charged at her.

Charleston flew at the demon.

Beheading it.

He grabbed Augusta's arm.

"Go!" he shouted.

A goblin tackled him to the ground.

Charleston punched the goblin. Breaking its jaw.

They had to go now. This battle was lost. The defensive line was broken.

"Fall back!" Charleston shouted.

He had no idea who was still alive to hear but this line was dead.

And unless they made it to the next defensive line they would all be dead in short order.

Even the wonderful woman he loved.

CHAPTER 15

Blood covered Augusta's face, hair and all her armour by the time she reached the Stone Circle. She really knew she shouldn't have stayed around to fight but she wanted to prove herself a fighter and Charleston had said that he loved her.

The stone circle was a lot darker than earlier and that wasn't only because it was night time. She could feel that something else was here too almost like a dark presence lurking in the growing shadows behind the stone seats that were arranged in a strange perfect circle.

Magic was hardly her area of expertise but she was seriously hoping she knew enough to get past and hopefully make the mountain trust her enough to reveal its secrets. If they were ever going to win against Sacaden she needed the power, knowledge and artefacts in this mountain.

The sound of shouting, slaughter and smashing of swords echoed up the valley so Augusta knew it was only a matter of time until the second line of defence fell to the enemy and then it would be the narrowest defence line that would hold Prison Rock in-between the state of freedom and annihilation.

Augusta had to hurry.

She went into the middle of the Stone Circle and sat on the floor. She knew that circles had power and as a woman she had innate magic even if she never used it or was able to use it.

Magic only went to gay men, all women and rarely (extremely rarely) straight men like Sacaden so Augusta was hoping the fact she was a woman might make the mountain trust her.

Nothing happened.

Augusta had no idea how to use magic but at the meeting earlier there had been a spare seat that she got the sense that it was powerful and even the ruler of Longmano sat there.

She stood up and went over to the stone seat that was the plainest, weakest and it certainly looked the least uncomfortable. Yet Augusta didn't care she wasn't a Queen for power, riches or anything besides the fact that she was here to protect her people.

The people and subjects she loved with all her heart.

A loud roar of a dragon ripped through the valley and Augusta was really glad that Cargo was trying to slow down the enemy advance.

But it was a stalling tactic at best. She had to hurry.

Augusta sat down on the stone seat and a sharp shard of rock stabbed into her back.

Then another shot into her neck.

Another shard shot into her bum.

Augusta took a long deep breath but she didn't care. She focused on the teachings that her father had gifted her one summer afternoon when they were walking in the Palace gardens. He told her that every moment of pain or discomfort is passing. Love is the only thing that never dies.

She nodded and she pushed her weight onto the sharp shards because she didn't care about the pain she was in.

She only cared about saving the innocent people dying in the mountain.

"You are definitely pure of heart," a voice said.

Augusta looked around but she couldn't see anyone.

"It's been a very, very long time since someone good and noble has sat on that seat. I still wasn't expecting *them* to make *you* Queen,"

Augusta wasn't really sure the owner of the voice liked her or not.

"What will you do with the knowledge I will give you?" the voice asked.

"I'll use the knowledge, power and artefacts you give me to protect the innocent. You can have them back forever if you want afterwards. Just please. Let me save these people,"

The voice laughed and Augusta had no idea why.

She was only speaking the truth.

"I admire fools like you. Always honest, always truthful and always good at heart. But you, you're different somehow I can sense you don't let others manipulate you,"

Augusta weakly smiled and the sharp shards were starting to pain her badly.

"Would you give your life for these people?"

"Yes," Augusta said without hesitation and she hadn't even realised that was her answer until it came out.

A very tall man with pointy, beautiful features appeared in front of her and he smiled.

"Relax Queen Augusta you will not be dying today and you have passed the test. Take my hand and I will reveal to you what the mountain has,"

The man extended his hand and Augusta wasn't sure about taking it.

Screams. Demonic laughter. War cries echoed up and down the valley and around the Stone Circle.

The enemy had claimed yet another victory.

Her time was up. Augusta took the man's hand and the world fell away from her.

CHAPTER 16

Charleston had absolutely no idea how many witches and wizards had survived the slaughter of the first line of defence. He knew that Augusta was safe for now but he seriously knew that if she failed they were all going to die.

Him and Owen stood with their swords out at the second line he had organised. Battered witches and wizards in dirt-covered robes stood next to him and around him.

The opening of this part of the valley was foul and awfully large. It was so much harder to defend but this was the narrowest point of the second-third of the valley that led to the Stone Circle. It wasn't a good option but it was the best location they had.

"Form a wall," Charleston said.

The witches and wizards around him looked so battered, tired and defeated that none of them wanted to do anything but they didn't have an option. Something they clearly missed.

A thunderstorm screamed around them and rain lashed down upon them.

The temperature dropped and the rain instantly became hail.

Then Charleston noticed that a witch that was allowing the hail to hit her was bleeding. The more the hail hit her the more blood dripped down her face.

All the hail seemed to focus on her for a moment.

The hail ripped the flesh off her. She screamed in agony as the hail stripped her of her skin, flesh and bones.

The hail smashed into all of them.

"Form a barrier!" Charleston shouted.

All the witches and wizards clicked their fingers and a ceiling of ice formed over them but then Charleston noticed all the magic users seemed drained, some knelt on the ground and others had immense gashes to their heads.

He didn't understand how magic worked but it was clear as day as that the ice ceiling was taking a hell of a lot of magic to maintain.

The foul laughter of goblins echoed around as Charleston watched their foul little footprints dance up and down on the ice ceiling.

The witches and wizards moaned in pain.

The goblins slammed their swords into the ice. The witches and wizards broke the concentration.

Goblins felt through.

Charleston flew forwards.

The hail was gone.

He swung his sword.

Beheading goblins.

Their laughter echoed around the valley.

A club smashed into Charleston.

Throwing him against the black rock.

The rock sliced Charleston's head.

He could barely think. His eyesight turned blurry.

He saw a witch rush over to him. she healed him.

The witch screamed in agony as she was turned to dust.

Sacaden punched Charleston.

Charleston fell sideways.

Collapsing to the floor.

Savannah's corpse stood over him. She was a zombie.

All around him witches and wizards screamed as they were murdered.

Charleston had lost yet another defence line.

Then all the goblins and demons and other creatures that dared to attack them disappeared and Sacaden's laughter filled the air.

Even Savannah's traitorous corpse slumped to the ground as Sacaden absorbed her magic.

Sacaden grabbed Charleston by the shoulders and forced him up. Charleston went straight over to Owen who was pointing his sword straight at Sacaden.

That's when Charleston realised him and Owen

were the only survivors. Sacaden and his monsters had murdered every single witch and wizard on Prison Rock.

"I believe in the power of a Last Stand. So Charleston and Owen run away to your final line of defence and I promise you only myself and my three new trolls will attack,"

Charleston didn't want to waste any time. If Sacaden was arrogant enough to give them time to prepare for a final attack then Charleston was going to take advantage of it.

He only hoped that Sacaden's arrogance was his downfall because the next time Sacaden saw him and precious Owen the wizard would kill them.

And Charleston hated to imagine what he would do to beautiful Augusta when he found her.

CHAPTER 17

When Augusta reappeared inside an awfully dark black stone chamber with six equally spaced burning torches hanging on the walls with a pitch dark ceiling and floor. She instantly knew that something was horrifically wrong and she only felt defeated, cold and so damn annoyed at herself.

"Where is everything?" Augusta asked.

She looked at the man with his pointy face that had led her down here probably by some magical version of teleportation.

The man smiled.

Augusta hated the man. He was clearly a spirit of some sort but this flat out wasn't funny in the slightest. The man she loved and his wonderful brother were fighting above them and they were about to die.

She had to save them.

"I thought you were taking me to the knowledge, power and artefacts of this place,"

The man nodded like that was the truest thing he had ever heard.

"I was going to take you there and I have," the man said.

Augusta shook her head. "There are no artefacts, powers or knowledge on Prison Rock is there,"

"Not in the way that you imagine,"

Augusta laughed. "I don't have time for this. My friends are dying out there,"

"Only your boyfriend and his brother are alive. Everyone else is dead including Jerry,"

Augusta was shocked. She had no idea how the hell Sacaden had managed to kill them all so quickly but this was awful. She had to be with them.

"Your dragon is already busy fighting off possessed dragons that Sacaden controls it is only a matter of time before he dies. Then your boyfriend and his brother dies too,"

Augusta fell against one of the rocky walls of the chamber. She had tried so damn hard to make sure everyone survived this but she was just another failure.

Maybe she wasn't actually good enough to be queen, maybe she was useless and maybe Jasper and Sacaden were the rightful rulers of the human lands.

No.

Augusta shook the stupid thought away and she looked at the man. As annoying as he was she absolutely refused to believe that he thought her down here to mock her.

"Who are you and what did you mean about the artefacts?" Augusta asked.

The man grinned. "I am the first king of Longmano, well actually of humanity,"

Augusta nodded. "Yes. King Jacobian ruled over the human lands for a thousand years but he was so greedy and corrupt and stupid that the regions of his country rebelled. That led to the creation of six kingdoms and then Jasper extended into two more countries creating the four kingdoms we know today,"

Jacobian bit his lip. "And the Gods and Goddesses killed me as punishment and so I am trapped on Prison Rock,"

Augusta gasped as she realised that he was the treasure. He would have been watching, learning and dealing with humanity for hundreds of thousands of years.

He absolutely had to know something that could help her.

"I never would have used any powerful artefacts anyway," Augusta said. "Please, what can I do to win?"

The man shook his head. "Ask me another question,"

"What can I do to help my friends live?"

The man nodded. "Believe in your power and unleash your magic. You have always known you have some and you put it down to you simply being a woman. You know that's a lie,"

Augusta looked down at her palm and small zaps of fire hopped out of her fingertips. She had already known she was a witch and he was right. Even Jerry had known it when he had first said she was like the people in the Stone Seats in more ways than one. She had always tried to blame it on the fact that she was a woman.

But she was a lot more than a woman. She was a witch and the time for hiding was over.

"Return me," Augusta said.

The man shrugged. "Return yourself witch,"

As he disappeared and she was left alone in the icy coldness of the chamber, fear gripped her.

Augusta had no idea how to escape and save the man she loved.

And she knew that every moment she was in here was another moment closer to his death.

And the moment the human world fell.

CHAPTER 18

Charleston seriously couldn't believe it as him and Owen stood in the Stone Circle and Sacaden had basically followed them here. This was where they were hoping to make a final stand and the damn wizard had silently followed them.

Charleston had at least wanted a few minutes to create some kind of plan with his brother about how to defeat Sacaden.

But Sacaden took off his black hood and Charleston bit his lip as he witnessed Sacaden's twisted face with the screaming faces of his victims constantly moving around.

Three trolls appeared behind Sacaden. Their skin covered in dragon scales and their smile and eyes and voice sounded so demonic. Each of them pounding a massive metal club against the ground.

"Kill them," Sacaden said.

The trolls shot forward.

Raising their clubs.

They swung at Charleston.
He leapt out the way.
Two trolls dashed towards Owen.
Charleston rushed over them.
The last troll swung his club.
Smashing Charleston.
Throwing him across the Stone Circle.
He slammed into them.
Shattering a stone seat.
The stones screamed in agony.
The stones reacted violently.
Stone shards rose up.
Launching themselves at the troll.
Ripping away dragon scales.
Charleston charged at the troll.
Charleston swung his sword.
The troll blocked him.
The troll screamed in rage.
Charleston's sword vibrated in his hands.
It didn't stop vibrating.
Charleston released it.
The sword flew towards the troll.

The troll used it as a toothpick. Before crushing it in its hands.

The troll roared at Charleston.
Charleston rushed over to Owen.
Two trolls were standing over him.
The trolls were about to crush him.
Charleston charged at them.
He leapt into the air.

Landing on the back of one troll.

Charleston climbed on it.

The trolls roared in confusion.

Charleston wrapped his legs round the neck of one troll.

He squeezed.

The troll tried to punch him away.

Charleston dodged it.

He kept squeezing.

The troll coughed.

It gasped for air.

Charleston kept squeezing.

The other trolls charged over.

The troll Charleston was choking collapsed.

Charleston jumped off.

He kicked the troll in the eye.

Killing it.

The other two trolls stopped dead in their tracks.

Owen jumped up.

Throwing his sword at the trolls.

The sword rammed into the eye of another troll.

The troll slammed onto Stone Circle.

The last troll looked at Sacaden like he was meant to do something and Charleston just shook his head when Sacaden snapped his fingers and the two trolls rose again but their movements were harsh, unrefined and now they were basically real trolls.

Except these two looked like they barely knew about to move or walk.

Magical energy wrapped around Charleston's

body. Owen hissed in pain. Charleston hated this magic he could barely move.

Charleston screamed in pain as it felt like he was being crushed.

"I came here for knowledge and power and some artefacts," Sacaden said as he stood in the centre of the Stone Circle.

Charleston hissed in pain as the magical force tightened around him.

"But now I am here I can sense those things are lies so I will murder you, Owen and Augusta and then I will conquer the entire world,"

Charleston wanted to say something but he couldn't move and he was in too much pain to speak.

"Release them," Augusta said as she walked into the Stone Circle.

Charleston was so glad to see her and she looked so sexy but he couldn't help but feel like she was different.

A flaming sword shot out of her hand and Charleston just grinned as he knew that Sacaden was done for.

He didn't know how. He knew only it was happening.

CHAPTER 19

Augusta seriously didn't care that she wasn't a powerful witch. She only cared about slaughtering Sacaden just like how he had murdered so many of her magical brothers and sisters today.

She stormed towards him. Her flaming sword in hand and all she wanted to do was kill him.

Augusta charged.

Sacaden looked so confused.

He clicked his fingers.

The trolls stormed towards her.

Augusta leapt into the air.

The trolls were too slow.

They swung at her.

Augusta launched fireballs at them.

They screamed.

They jerked backwards.

The swings of their clubs were off.

Augusta clicked her fingers.

The trolls' clubs became raging infernos.

The trolls charged towards her.

Augusta hadn't expected that.

She dashed away.

The troll grabbed one of her legs.

She screamed.

Augusta launched a fireball at the troll.

It didn't work.

The other trolls came over.

They grabbed her arms.

They were pulling her in different directions.

She hissed.

Her bones protested.

Her joints roared in agony.

Augusta screamed.

Fire shot out of her mouth. Hands. Toes.

The trolls shot away.

Their hands on fire.

The smell of smouldering flesh filled the air.

The trolls were in chaos.

Augusta thrusted out her hands.

Torrents of rageful black fire roared out of them.

Engulfing the trolls.

Burning them to death.

The trolls were no more.

"Stop that," Sacaden said. "Or I will crush them,"

Augusta didn't know how she knew it but she could guess that Sacaden was scared of her but she knew her magic wasn't endless. A pounding headache corkscrewed across her head.

She couldn't use her magic continuously.

Augusta shot out her hands.

No magic or fire came out.

Sacaden laughed at her as a magical force wrapped around her and started crushing her.

Augusta focused on beautiful sexy Charleston with his fit sexy body, handsome face and amazing personality. He was just so damn kind, wonderful and everything she had ever wanted in a man.

She couldn't die. He had told her he loved her but she hadn't done the same.

She wasn't going to allow some dickhead like Sacaden to kill her before that had happened.

Then Augusta realised exactly what the man Jacobian had mentioned earlier. There weren't any artefacts, powers or knowledge in here like she had imagined and she hadn't realised exactly what he had said either about her.

She needed to believe in herself.

She could and would beat Sacaden because she was a queen and she wasn't dying today.

Augusta thrusted out her arms and Sacaden stumbled back like a little old man and she stormed over to him.

She kicked him in the jaw. Three teeth flew out.

"How?" Sacaden asked truly terrified.

Charleston and Owen joined her and Augusta so hardly wanted to kiss Charleston but she had to kill Sacaden first.

As much as Augusta didn't want to kill him, she

was going to have to.

Charleston looked at Augusta and he smiled and she just went over to him and hugged the man she had loved for so long.

Sacaden slowly stood up and he seemed so weak now.

Augusta shook her head at him. "You're weak. Your magic's weakness is simply something you will never understand,"

Sacaden stomped his foot on the ground. "I have everything. I have the chieftains, I have magic and I have an entire country,"

Augusta laughed. "Yes but you don't have love. Love is your weakness and my love for my people, Owen and Charleston will always be stronger than you,"

Sacaden screamed in rage.

Immense balls of fire formed in his hands.

A dragon's tail smashed into Sacaden's body and killed him.

A few moments later, Cargo gently landed in the middle of the Stone Circle and looked around like this was a brand-new holiday destination he had just arrived at.

"What did I miss everyone?" Cargo asked.

Augusta just laughed. The battle was over and she truly loved her friends more than anything else in the entire world.

CHAPTER 20

Charleston was completely amazed over the next few days as the true horror of Sacaden's work was revealed, and he was even more amazed, dazzled and stunned by how the love of his life handled it. Augusta was definitely a beautiful, righteous and fair queen that he truly loved.

After Sacaden's defeat, Charleston had expected Augusta to kill the chieftains that had allied themselves with the tyrant that had threatened the people she loved, but he was surprised that she actually just wanted to talk to them.

The two of them met the chieftains in a beautiful meadow with wildflowers growing and blowing in the wind and the smell of wonderful roses filled the air.

Charleston was sure the chieftains were going to kill them, but Augusta spoke to them and they actually listened and within ten minutes she accepted that the Chieftains wanted what was best for their people and Charleston had to admit that they weren't actually as monstrous as he believed.

So Augusta offered them land but they rejected her and they simply wanted to become her subjects, only loyal to her and they would instead set up their own towns in her name.

Charleston was still amazed that total strangers liked Augusta enough to take a chance on that.

Of course one or two tribes didn't like the idea of being ruled by Augusta but before she could give permission for the tribes to leave her kingdoms (including Longmano) the other tribes killed them. Thankfully not in her name.

Even Lordo had been given a job opportunity to continue his diplomatic work but he fled to the south along with all the foul monsters.

As Charleston leant against the perfectly warm cream stone walls of the Longmanoian palace, he focused on the wonderful stone houses, businesses and bakeries that tons of happy people were talking around and hugging friends again.

There were a group of young men and women, all school friends it seemed, and they were singing and dancing and hugging each other. Because they were alive and Charleston had spoken to some of them earlier and they were just so happy that Augusta had saved them.

Charleston was slightly impressed that he wasn't jealous and it was him, Owen and a bunch of sadly dead witches and wizards that had also played a part in saving them. But he didn't want to correct them, because Augusta really was amazing.

Large black, brown and white horses pulled wooden carriages up and down the wide open street and bumped over the cobblestone road as business returned to normal.

Or as normal as it could possibly be.

As Owen wearing a very fine white tunic that made him look almost regal stood next to him, Charleston was just delighted in how Longmano was starting to recover. The military, Augusta and Charleston had all managed to push back the creatures to the border.

And now Augusta had ordered a brand-new military base to be built. One that would form a Great Wall over the southern border to make sure the creatures, trolls and demons of the south could never invade again.

She had also thankfully ordered one to be created in the North as well to keep the orks out. It had been the sacrifice of the wizards and witches that had apparently given her the idea.

"You look beautiful Owen," Charleston said.

Owen grinned and it was the sort of grin that Charleston hadn't seen his brother have… for ages maybe ever. It was the sort of smile a teenage boy got when they were in love.

Charleston had maybe seen Owen have it once when he was very young when he used to go to school as an early teenager, but then that was when his father had found out that Owen was gay. Then the abuse started and he really hadn't seen Owen smile like that for years.

Charleston just hugged him.

"How are you?" Charleston asked.

He was partly expecting Owen to cry or something but he didn't. His eyes turned a little wet but Charleston just forgot sometimes how amazingly strong his precious brother was.

"I endure," Owen said. "I killed father two years ago. He cannot hurt me and love is out there for me. As it is you,"

Charleston nodded about that. As soon as Augusta was done setting up a Lord Governor for the Longmano region of her kingdom, they had to return to Octogi and then Charleston was going to properly confess his love for her because it was exactly what he needed to do.

He couldn't waste any more time not loving her and he knew that she felt the exact same way. And that really did make him feel warm, fuzzy and wonderful inside and out.

CHAPTER 21

As much as Augusta absolutely loved travelling to amazing Longmano, visiting Lordigo for a week and then returning to her native Octogi, she had to admit there was no place like home whatsoever.

She stood in a different part of the Royal Gardens with thick, dense black trees covered in rough sharp bark surrounding them and she was just focused on a small dangerously thin plant with a black stem, black petals and a blood-red centre.

Her father called it *The Queen* and there was a large white circle around it that glowed bright white to make sure no one dared to cross the line, because it was meant to be a very deadly plant.

The sound of birds singing, servants and gardening talking in the distance and quiet footsteps coming up behind her made her smile, because her wonderful world really was back to normal again.

The air was amazingly fresh, crisp and even with a slight hint of damp that was almost revitalising after the battle, that left the delightful flavour of spring sandwiches in forests like she had done when she was a child with her mother, brother and father.

Now she was the only one left.

She was thankfully queen of yet another kingdom and that had solved a lot of her problems. The great people of Longmano now had a ruler that loved, protected and would always act in their best interests. And because of that little fact they had offered to help the other regions of her growing kingdom.

The Longmanoians were shopaholics so Lordigo's industries were thriving once again and there were having to fulfil more and more orders by the day. And it even didn't matter now that Jasper had cut off trade with her other kingdoms because Octogi, Longmano and Lordigo all had more than enough businesses and industries to provide each other with everything they needed.

Jasper had lost whatever political war it had been trying to fight.

It was even better than the Longmanoians could free up their army because of the wall so her armies had combined and managed to push out the orks. Now The Great Northern Wall was being built to make sure the orks could never ever return to the human lands ever again.

Of course they would still need to be defended but hopefully not as much.

Two very strong, manly and perfect arms wrapped around her and she kissed them as

Charleston turned her around.

"Are you actually doing this?" Augusta asked grinning.

Charleston shrugged. "We've both confessed our love for each other. We both do love each other. And the people love you and me, they won't care that a Queen and a servant are dating,"

Augusta laughed. "I have never thought of you as a servant,"

"I know," Charleston said kissing her.

Augusta groaned in pleasure in the most un-regal way possible as the softness, manliness and taste of his lips were far better than she ever could have wished for.

Charleston pushed her away. "I do just have to ask one question though. When you killed Sacaden, did you become the Goblin King?"

Augusta clicked her fingers. "Not exactly. You see one night after Sacaden was killed I met up with the goblins and made them a deal they were all too happy to accept. They promised me in exchange for returning the Rite of Kingship to their own species, they would never ever return to the human lands,"

"Please tell me you didn't have that fat tall one King? I never liked him and he did threaten to gut me,"

Augusta laughed and kissed him again. He certainly didn't need to know that was exactly what she had done.

Augusta started moving further and further back

so she pushed Charleston away and made sure she hadn't crossed the circle and she thankfully hadn't. Only just.

"What is that plant?" Charleston asked.

"My father's favourite and I think it's rather symbolic of Jasper considering it's called *The Queen*,"

Augusta picked up a broken piece of bark on the ground and threw it past the circle.

The Queen snatched the bark. Devouring it.

Within a second that piece of bark had been completely destroyed.

"You are a deadly one," Charleston said wrapping his arms around her.

Augusta nodded. "Exactly. Once my rule is established truly in Longmano we must turn our attention to claiming Jasper. Its armies are already moving to our borders, Cargo reports that his dragon kin are being murdered and Jasper will strike us soon,"

Charleston didn't say a word and only hugged her tighter, and Augusta understood exactly why.

Jasper was the most powerful kingdom in terms of trade, military and politics in the human lands and to be honest, even the elves and dwarves couldn't put a candle up against Jasper.

That single country was a threat to all of them and time was seriously running out to defeat Jasper before Jasper wiped them out.

But that was tomorrow's problem and they probably had a good month or two before Jasper was ready, so Augusta turned around and hugged and kissed the wonderful man she loved.

The man she had been longing for, for so long and as they kissed more and more she certainly knew they were going to make up for a lot of lost time.

And she was going to love every single second of it.

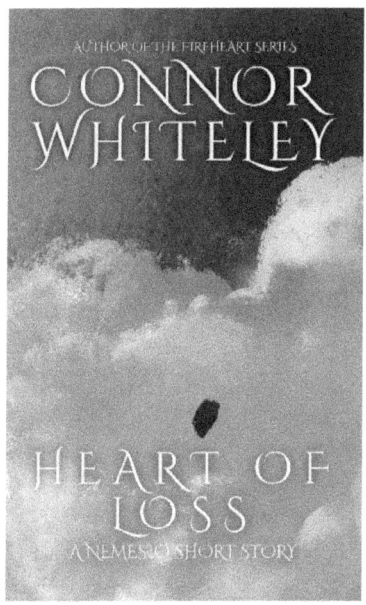

GET YOUR FREE AND EXCLUSIVE SHORT STORY NOW! LEARN ABOUT NEMESIO'S PAST!

https://www.subscribepage.com/fireheart

Keep up to date with exclusive deals on Connor Whiteley's Books, as well as the latest news about new releases and so much more!

Sign up for the Grab a Book and Chill Monthly newsletter, and you'll get one **FREE** ebook just for signing up: Agents of The Emperor Collection.

Sign Up Now!

https://dl.bookfunnel.com/f4p5xkprbk

About the author:

Connor Whiteley is the author of over 60 books in the sci-fi fantasy, nonfiction psychology and books for writer's genre and he is a Human Branding Speaker and Consultant.

He is a passionate warhammer 40,000 reader, psychology student and author.

Who narrates his own audiobooks and he hosts The Psychology World Podcast.

All whilst studying Psychology at the University of Kent, England.

Also, he was a former Explorer Scout where he gave a speech to the Maltese President in August 2018 and he attended Prince Charles' 70th Birthday Party at Buckingham Palace in May 2018.

Plus, he is a self-confessed coffee lover!

Other books by Connor Whiteley:
Bettie English Private Eye Series
A Very Private Woman
The Russian Case
A Very Urgent Matter
A Case Most Personal
Trains, Scots and Private Eyes
The Federation Protects

Lord of War Origin Trilogy:
Not Scared Of The Dark
Madness
Burn Them All

The Fireheart Fantasy Series
Heart of Fire
Heart of Lies
Heart of Prophecy
Heart of Bones
Heart of Fate

City of Assassins (Urban Fantasy)
City of Death
City of Marytrs
City of Pleasure
City of Power

Agents of The Emperor
Return of The Ancient Ones
Vigilance
Angels of Fire
Kingmaker
The Eight
The Lost Generation
Hunt
Emperor's Council
Speaker of Treachery
Birth Of The Empire
Terraforma

The Rising Augusta Fantasy Adventure Series
Rise To Power
Rising Walls
Rising Force
Rising Realm

Lord Of War Trilogy (Agents of The Emperor)
Not Scared Of The Dark
Madness
Burn It All Down

Gay Romance Novellas
Breaking, Nursing, Repairing A Broken Heart
Jacob And Daniel
Fallen For A Lie
Spying And Weddings

The Garro Series- Fantasy/Sci-fi
GARRO: GALAXY'S END
GARRO: RISE OF THE ORDER
GARRO: END TIMES
GARRO: SHORT STORIES
GARRO: COLLECTION
GARRO: HERESY
GARRO: FAITHLESS
GARRO: DESTROYER OF WORLDS
GARRO: COLLECTIONS BOOK 4-6
GARRO: MISTRESS OF BLOOD
GARRO: BEACON OF HOPE
GARRO: END OF DAYS

Winter Series- Fantasy Trilogy Books
WINTER'S COMING
WINTER'S HUNT
WINTER'S REVENGE
WINTER'S DISSENSION

Miscellaneous:
RETURN
FREEDOM
SALVATION
Reflection of Mount Flame
The Masked One
The Great Deer
English Independence

OTHER SHORT STORIES BY CONNOR WHITELEY

Mystery Short Story Collections
Criminally Good Stories Volume 1: 20 Detective Mystery Short Stories
Criminally Good Stories Volume 2: 20 Private Investigator Short Stories
Criminally Good Stories Volume 3: 20 Crime Fiction Short Stories
Criminally Good Stories Volume 4: 20 Science Fiction and Fantasy Mystery Short Stories
Criminally Good Stories Volume 5: 20 Romantic Suspense Short Stories

Mystery Short Stories:
Protecting The Woman She Hated
Finding A Royal Friend

Our Woman In Paris
Corrupt Driving
A Prime Assassination
Jubilee Thief
Jubilee, Terror, Celebrations
Negative Jubilation
Ghostly Jubilation
Killing For Womenkind
A Snowy Death
Miracle Of Death
A Spy In Rome
The 12:30 To St Pancreas
A Country In Trouble
A Smokey Way To Go
A Spicy Way To GO
A Marketing Way To Go
A Missing Way To Go
A Showering Way To Go
Poison In The Candy Cane
Christmas Innocence
You Better Watch Out
Christmas Theft
Trouble In Christmas
Smell of The Lake
Problem In A Car
Theft, Past and Team
Embezzler In The Room

A Strange Way To Go
A Horrible Way To Go
Ann Awful Way To Go
An Old Way To Go
A Fishy Way To Go
A Pointy Way To Go
A High Way To Go
A Fiery Way To Go
A Glassy Way To Go
A Chocolatey Way To Go
Kendra Detective Mystery Collection Volume 1
Kendra Detective Mystery Collection Volume 2
Stealing A Chance At Freedom
Glassblowing and Death
Theft of Independence
Cookie Thief
Marble Thief
Book Thief
Art Thief
Mated At The Morgue
The Big Five Whoopee Moments
Stealing An Election
Mystery Short Story Collection Volume 1
Mystery Short Story Collection Volume 2
Criminal Performance

Candy Detectives
Key To Birth In The Past

<u>Science Fiction Short Stories:</u>
Temptation
Superhuman Autospy
Blood In The Redwater
All Is Dust
Vigil
Emperor Forgive Us
Their Brave New World
Gummy Bear Detective
The Candy Detective
What Candies Fear
The Blurred Image
Shattered Legions
The First Rememberer
Life of A Rememberer
System of Wonder
Lifesaver
Remarkable Way She Died
The Interrogation of Annabella Stormic
Blade of The Emperor
Arbiter's Truth
Computation of Battle
Old One's Wrath
Puppets and Masters

RISING WALLS

Ship of Plague
Interrogation
Edge of Failure
One Way Choice
Acceptable Losses
Balance of Power
Good Idea At The Time
Escape Plan
Escape In The Hesitation
Inspiration In Need
Singing Warriors
Knowledge is Power
Killer of Polluters
Climate of Death
The Family Mailing Affair
Defining Criminality
The Martian Affair
A Cheating Affair
The Little Café Affair
Mountain of Death
Prisoner's Fight
Claws of Death
Bitter Air
Honey Hunt
Blade On A Train
<u>Fantasy Short Stories:</u>
City of Snow

City of Light
City of Vengeance
Dragons, Goats and Kingdom
Smog The Pathetic Dragon
Don't Go In The Shed
The Tomato Saver
The Remarkable Way She Died
The Bloodied Rose
Asmodia's Wrath
Heart of A Killer
Emissary of Blood
Dragon Coins
Dragon Tea
Dragon Rider
Sacrifice of the Soul
Heart of The Flesheater
Heart of The Regent
Heart of The Standing
Feline of The Lost
Heart of The Story
City of Fire
Awaiting Death

All books in 'An Introductory Series':
Careers In Psychology
Psychology of Suicide
Dementia Psychology
Forensic Psychology of Terrorism And Hostage-Taking
Forensic Psychology of False Allegations
Year In Psychology
BIOLOGICAL PSYCHOLOGY 3RD EDITION
COGNITIVE PSYCHOLOGY THIRD EDITION
SOCIAL PSYCHOLOGY- 3RD EDITION
ABNORMAL PSYCHOLOGY 3RD EDITION
PSYCHOLOGY OF RELATIONSHIPS- 3RD EDITION
DEVELOPMENTAL PSYCHOLOGY 3RD EDITION
HEALTH PSYCHOLOGY
RESEARCH IN PSYCHOLOGY
A GUIDE TO MENTAL HEALTH AND TREATMENT AROUND THE WORLD- A GLOBAL LOOK AT DEPRESSION
FORENSIC PSYCHOLOGY
THE FORENSIC PSYCHOLOGY OF THEFT, BURGLARY AND OTHER

CRIMES AGAINST PROPERTY
CRIMINAL PROFILING: A FORENSIC PSYCHOLOGY GUIDE TO FBI PROFILING AND GEOGRAPHICAL AND STATISTICAL PROFILING.
CLINICAL PSYCHOLOGY FORMULATION IN PSYCHOTHERAPY
PERSONALITY PSYCHOLOGY AND INDIVIDUAL DIFFERENCES
CLINICAL PSYCHOLOGY REFLECTIONS VOLUME 1
CLINICAL PSYCHOLOGY REFLECTIONS VOLUME 2
Clinical Psychology Reflections Volume 3
CULT PSYCHOLOGY
Police Psychology

A Psychology Student's Guide To University
How Does University Work?
A Student's Guide To University And Learning
University Mental Health and Mindset

www.ingramcontent.com/pod-product-compliance
Lightning Source LLC
LaVergne TN
LVHW012114070526
838202LV00056B/5727